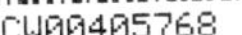

Shifted Code

By Elijah Frederick

'Shifted Code'

Published in Great Britain by

Elijah Frederick

First Printing: 2018

Acknowledgement

I express my deep gratitude to my family who have encouraged me to write this book. The best support I had did not come from a manual, but the most important person in my life, my mum. Thank you mum! I would also like to thank Abi and Oyehmi Begho who have been so supportive and have enabled me to publish this book.

Contents

Chapter 1

It was 2pm and time for the last lesson of the day. Tadeo ambled along at the back of the line, which is where he belonged in the eyes of his classmates. He didn't have many friends and it was all because of Nathan and his gang.

They were a group of bullies who terrorised the school, especially anyone smaller or smarter than them.

Luckily, Nathan and his friends seemed to be ignoring Tadeo today, but other days they would tease him, calling him a freak, big-head and many more hurtful names. He didn't know how to respond and whenever he got annoyed it just drove them to continue. It wasn't just those boys, the whole class would join in and make fun of him, even the ones who were supposed to be his friends. They teased him just to fit in.

This constant bullying made Tadeo feel very insecure and alone. He didn't know who to tell or talk to. Once or twice he thought about telling his parents but imagined they would feel disappointed in him for not sticking up for himself, so he kept it all bottled up inside.

The bell rang, and the class entered the computer room, Nathan and his friends sat at the back of the classroom. One of them whispered in Nathan's ear and laughed loudly, forgetting that the teacher, Mrs Crilger, was right there.

Mrs Crilger was a nice teacher but very strict. She cleared her throat, waited for silence and gave the class clear instructions on what the task for the lesson was. They were to make a computer game with a partner and she immediately began pairing the class up until finally there were four students left to be paired: Nathan, two of his friends and Tadeo. Mrs Crilger's face said it all; she was puzzled about who to put with who.

Making up her mind, she thought that

this would be a good test for Nathan. She put Nathan's two friends together and left Tadeo with Nathan. Tadeo sighed heavily, bowing his head. This was his worst nightmare. Nathan kissed his teeth, walked over to Tadeo and took a seat next to him. He knew working with Tadeo would be bad for his reputation.

Tadeo started the task eagerly, brainstorming some ideas for games. Seeing what Tadeo was writing, Nathan took the piece of paper and wrote an idea. To his surprise, Tadeo thought that Nathan's idea was a good one, it was a simple idea but adventurous and fun.

Tadeo began typing up their assignment, while Nathan was sneakily playing on his phone. Nathan then pulled out a can of Coca-Cola from his bag, even though he knew he wasn't allowed fizzy drinks in class.

Mrs Crilger, who was working on her computer, looked up, happy to see her students working peacefully, then she noticed Nathan and angrily walked across the room and stood behind him.

She ordered Nathan to give her the Coca-Cola. He disobeyed and accidently spilt the drink on the keyboard just as Tadeo was entering the code for the villain of their game.

The computer started to make a low humming sound, smoke began to appear and then sparks flew up out of the computer.

The fire alarm sounded, and everyone was evacuated from the building. As the class was walking to the playground Mrs Crilger told the children to finish off their game, with their partners as homework and to submit it in a week's time.

Tadeo and Nathan didn't want to work together but knew that they had to otherwise they would fail their end-of-year computing assessment. Tadeo didn't want to fail, Nathan on the other hand didn't mind but wanted to do well just so he could get the latest hand-held console, the Switch Sphere, which his parents had promised him if he passed.

One Sunday, Tadeo invited Nathan to his house while his parents were at a very important meeting, talking to the council about pollution. As Nathan walked up to the door he was shocked at the size of Tadeo's house. It looked like a mansion!

He rang the door and Tadeo slowly opened it.

"Hello Nathan," Tadeo greeted him.

"Dude, your house is so big, your parents must be rich. Right?" Nathan questioned.

"Well, not rich, they just have good jobs. My mum is the director of a spa, and my dad works in a bank. What do your parents do?" Tadeo enquired.

Nathan didn't respond, he barged Tadeo out of the way.

"Woah, cool!" Nathan exclaimed.

"You have to take off your shoes," Tadeo said alarmed. "My parents will kill me!"

"Like I care, that's your problem."

"The only reason you're here is because we're doing this project!" Tadeo yelled at him.

Ignoring Tadeo, Nathan didn't take his shoes off, he began exploring. He immediately dashed down the hallway and stopped when he saw a room to his left. Noticing a flat screen TV, he entered the room. He was impressed. Tadeo was close behind and followed Nathan into the next room to make sure he didn't cause any trouble.

In this room Nathan saw shelves and shelves of books. It was like Tadeo's family had their own library. He saw that there was a number engraved in the wood at the top of the shelves. Nathan pointed at one of the numbers and turned to Tadeo.

"That's how old I was when I read those books," Tadeo explained. Nathan looked bored;

he wasn't a big fan of reading and swiftly left the room looking for one that had more fun things to do.

Tadeo directed Nathan to his room. As he entered Tadeo's room, Nathan noticed the Gamechip 64 which Tadeo's parents had given him for scoring the highest mark in his class in the practice SAT paper.

"We best start to work, yeah," Tadeo said. He pulled out an A3 piece of paper and started planning out their game for the project. Every now and again Nathan contributed an idea, however, he was mostly admiring Tadeo's Gamechip 64.

When Tadeo and Nathan had completed their plan for the game they logged on to Scratch, the software their teacher gave them to build their computer game. They had to create a brand-new game as the one that Tadeo started in class was deleted from the computer after the Coca-Cola fire incident.

Nathan and Tadeo worked on their game and soon were on the final codes for the villains. Nathan suggested that in their game the villains should be able to move up, down, left and right with a speed of 1/10 (the slowest speed you can program). Tadeo imported the code and with that last code they were finished with their game.

Tadeo thought they had worked well together and said, "thanks for coming over Nathan," but was disappointed when Nathan replied:

"The only thing good about this place was the Gamechip 64!" Nathan picked up his bag, walked down the hallway and slammed the front door behind him without saying goodbye.

When Nathan left, Tadeo tested out their new game, it was good, but he felt it needed to be a bit more challenging, so he decided to edit the villains. He improved the computer code so one of the villains could summon evil minions.

"Perfect!" he thought, "much better!"

Transferring the game from Scratch onto the Gamechip 64, Tadeo touched it and with a sudden flash he was drawn into the USB stick like dust sucked into a vacuum cleaner.

Chapter 2

Very rapidly Tadeo was tumbling through a vortex. He noticed from the corner of his eye little computer codes, the ones he had created, were rushing past him in the vortex.

Seeing little rays of light Tadeo found hope that he was safe. Eventually the light got closer and closer to him. Covering his eyes Tadeo went through the light and landed roughly on his back. Tadeo got up, brushed himself off, checking to make sure he wasn't hurt. He looked around, afraid, wondering where he could be. He realised he was in a forest.

Where is this? How did I get here? Tadeo asked himself.

Observing his every move, a figure from above was watching over him from a bird's eye view.

Feeling afraid and as though he was being watched, Tadeo turned around but saw nothing there. He took a few steps and turned around again. The more he looked back the more he became uneasy. Finally, he heard the breeze rustling through pine needles.

"Whoever is there you should come out slowly."

"Calm down, no one here will hurt you," a voice spoke softly.

"Who is that?"

Jumping down from the tree, a masked man grabbed his arm and dragged Tadeo towards a shelter which was made from thick branches stuck firmly in the mud.

"Help me! Can anyone hear me? Please help me!" Tadeo cried as loudly as he could.

"I am helping you! Now, hold the noise. Got it?" the man said angrily.

"Who are you? What do you want with me?"

"Silence," the man shouted. Noticeably,

inside the shelter, the sharpened branches were slanted all around the hut, which was designed to intimidate any intruders. The masked man knew his way around very well. He entered the hut by slipping through a narrow spot between two of the deadly branches and signalled for Tadeo to follow him.

Tadeo was hesitant to follow him but had no choice, he was terrified and alone.

"Come on then, what are you waiting for?" the man asked irritably.

"Why should I trust you?" Tadeo asked.

"Just come in, quickly!" he replied.

"No! Why I should trust you?" Tadeo

repeated.

"I am trying to help you," the masked man pleaded.

Tadeo was still unsure, a conflict grew within him.

"Okay fine, it's you and the wolves then," the masked man said.

"W…W…wolves, like predator wolves?" Tadeo's voice trembled. "I'm not the fighting type of person so I am going to come in with you now."

"Wise choice boy," the masked man smiled.

Tadeo was able to fit through the narrow

spot between the two lethal branches. Entering the branch hut Tadeo saw another person arranging a couple of sticks into a pyramid type stack.

"Hey, Barboach, go get us a small batch of logs, these branches are useless for creating a fire," the other person said.

"But Clitho the sun is setting, and the pack of wolves will be out soon."

"O yeah, I forgot about that, but how could I?" Clitho spoke softly.

"I know, those wolves are despicable, they think anything they see they can kill and eat." Barboach hung his cloak up on a hook.

Tadeo couldn't believe his eyes, he thought he was dreaming. Barboach was a weasel! His jaw dropped, a talking weasel - I must be dreaming, he thought. "Is this for real, a weasel…" Tadeo began to ask.

"Have you never seen a weasel before?" Barboach asked.

"No, no I have, just never talked to one… in English."

Clitho laughed and Barboach smiled. The three of them exchanged a look of friendship but Tadeo still knew he was an outsider. Keeping dead silent in the corner of the hut for a couple of minutes Tadeo couldn't help but to listen to their plans.

"So, we have searched this area three times and still nothing. What do we do Clitho?"

"I don't know; but if we ever want to leave here we have got to find the flag."

Tadeo stood up, walked around the fire and saw that they had drawn a map in the dust.

"But on my way to your hut it was like every single blade of grass was replaced by a flag." Tadeo laughed.

"Yeah, we get that, but one flag is the exit flag," Clitho explained.

"Exit flag?" Tadeo was completely confused.

"You are in the Forest of Flags; legends say that one flag is the exit flag and that flag should be placed on the legendary tree stump. No one has found the exit flag yet, and those who fail to do so get cursed and live their lives for eternity like ghosts, and the ghosts cannot interact with the people that enter the forest of flags," Barboach told Tadeo.

"Wow! So, you guys are plan…" Tadeo began.

"Planning it out, yes we are, but we have been smart about it unlike everyone that has been cursed," Clitho interrupted.

"Well, I am glad to be with you guys,"

said Tadeo, trying to feel more relaxed and not like an outsider.

"Thanks," Clitho replied.

"Yeah, thanks," Barboach repeated. "But we have found a clue. It reads:

Cross the river

You will find two parallel trees

The one exactly between them

Guarded by a dog decorated in fleas

We have crossed the river countless times and have found no dog guarding a flag."

"Can I think about the clue. I think I can work it out.

"Okay, see you in the morning Tadeo,"

"Goodnight my new friend."

Tadeo then remembered he had a spare pair of glasses in his pocket,

"Yes, ok" he whispered.

He examined the small piece of paper but couldn't find anything. Hours passed and Tadeo was about to give up as the sun was beginning to rise. He knew he didn't have much time and he didn't want to disappoint his new friends.

Trying as hard as he could Tadeo scanned the paper countless times but found nothing. Tadeo felt so defeated. In frustration, he scrunched up the piece of paper and threw it into the fire in anger, but immediately regretted doing this. Looking on the bright side, he remembered the clue by heart since he had been reading it for so long.

Suddenly, out of the fire, emerged some writing in the smoke:

You must take the flag at midnight

But beware you will get such a fright

It was amazing! Tadeo was happy that he had figured it out, but the smile was wiped off his face as he remembered that wolves are out at night. There was no point going back to sleep, Tadeo thought. He was hungry and wondered where he could get something to eat. He thought he could get something for his new friends too.

He noticed a little area that had eggs, some dried bacon and sausage hanging near the basket.

What could he give Barboach? Tadeo wondered.

Clitho and Barboach were woken by the smell of food which was on their hand-made plates. Tadeo had caught a frog and a small rat and placed it on some leaves for Barboach. He found a pan and fried sausages, some bacon, and eggs for himself and Clitho.

"Wow, Tadeo this is delicious," Clitho complimented him.

"Yeah, good, the rat and frog have a nice flavour, you make a good hunter!" Barboach admitted.

"And guess what? I have some good news. I know why you guys haven't found the flag yet, it is because the flag and the dog only appear at night."

"Tadeo you are a walking computer," Barboach was shocked he had figured it out.

"Yeah, you are a genius," Clitho added.

"Thanks, Clitho," Tadeo replied.

They both smiled at each other with Barboach stuffing the tail of the rat into his mouth.

"We need a plan for how we're going to get the flag," Clitho told them.

"I've already got one guys," Barboach said once he had finished his brunch.

"I think we should get some rest so we can have some energy for tonight," Tadeo suggested.

"Good idea," Clitho said.

As night fell, the three friends had gotten some rest and they started to put their plan into action. They blew out the fire, but they weren't in pitch black darkness as they had a stick torch.

Following Clitho and Barboach, Tadeo saw the river in the distance so he got behind a bush while Barboach and Clitho were climbing the trees.

It was time to put the first part of their plan into action. Tadeo had built a robotic squirrel a few months ago for a class project. He still had it in his bag, the squirrel could fold in and out of its shape.

Taking the robotic squirrel and its remote control from his bag, Tadeo made the squirrel move across the river. They were going to use this device to trap the dog. Like a car chase the squirrel was running from the dog, the plan was working. Although the dog was falling for the plan, the only reason the squirrel looked believable was because it was dark.

Swinging like monkeys, Clitho and Barboach swung onto some vines, until Clitho landed onto a branch that was too short and slipped and fell into the river.

"Clitho! Noooooooooooo!" Tadeo screamed out while courageously diving into the river.

The river surged around Tadeo's body, encasing him with its ice-cold water. He began to move his arms, pulling himself through the clear frigid river. At first the water on Tadeo's face felt cold but as he was fighting the tide to save his friend it felt like he was being bitten.

His skin began to sting like bees on his face. Ignoring the pain, he continued, he had to save his friend.

Spotting a body, Tadeo grabbed it by the arm, firmly gripping a hand that he prayed was Clitho's. As he came out of the water Tadeo saw that he had just saved Clitho's life. Doing what he had been taught from health class he managed to hear a heartbeat from Clitho's chest.

Meanwhile, Barboach managed to get the flag and get away with it while the dog was still distracted. With Tadeo holding Clitho's arm and Barboach holding the other they all ran to the legendary tree stump with the dog running closely behind them. Distance and pressure meant nothing to them, their legs were still moving, though they felt like all their muscles had gone to sleep.

"Come on, we are almost there!" a resilient Barboach ran with an arm of Clitho's around his neck

"Where is it?" Tadeo asked

"Our hut is straight ahead so it should be near."

Out of breath, each gasping for air, they made it to the legendary tree stump, they all grabbed the flag and hurriedly placed it on the stump. Then, like a slam dunk, they jumped and with full power they placed it on the tree only to find themselves being sucked into the tree like metal to a magnet.

Chapter 3

In an instant Tadeo, Barboach and Clitho were in a desert. Tadeo knew now exactly where he was - inside of his own game!

The USB stick must have transferred me into the game when I was transferring the data he thought, just as he blacked out.

A couple of hours had passed, the huge golden sun rose, and its rays shone on Tadeo.

The desert was punctuated by the shadowy silhouettes of the cacti and the cruel sun beat down with great force. The lizards took shelter in the shadows of the rocks where the sand was not hot enough to roast them.

The painful sound of Barboach screaming awoke Tadeo from his unconscious state.

"Barboach, he is conscious again," Clitho joyfully exclaimed.

"You have been out for hours," Barboach told him.

"Where are we?" Tadeo asked

Looking around, Tadeo could see why Barboach had been screaming. Barboach was barefoot and the desert was covered in prickles, it was like needles had covered the floor and the pain seared through his skin.

Rising from the floor, with sand in his hair, Tadeo rubbed his eyes. With the sticky air and the heat Tadeo was sweating intensely.

Out of nowhere the sun's rays acted like lasers and cracked the floor, walls shot up like a tree. Before they all knew it, they were separated.

Calling for Clitho, Tadeo heard a faint voice reply, he assumed it was Clitho. Without thinking Tadeo rushed into the wall trying to knock it over. He tried and tried and tried, if anything the wall was knocking Tadeo backwards.

He couldn't do it anymore, his arm felt as weak as a feather. Looking up, at what was supposed to be the sky, in sorrow, Tadeo only saw a countdown on a digital clock.

This he didn't program into his game; puzzled he just kept on walking forward, then left, then right. Tadeo went every which way until he was dizzy and reached a dead end. His legs couldn't support his body weight anymore and he collapsed.

Tadeo had reached rock bottom! The moment Tadeo hit the floor, his small spark of hope extinguished. Like an oven the sun began baking his brain, while he lay on the floor.

A vague voice caught Tadeo's ear, he arose and followed it. As if the voice was talking directly to Tadeo, the same phrase repeated in his head.

The voice was like a trail Tadeo was following. It led him to an old man whom he was about to crash into, but he immediately halted just before that could happen. Noticeably, the man was in a yoga position but was in the air! A levitating man - wow! It was a bit too much for Tadeo to deal with.

Like a conductor's hand motion, the old man's hand waved up and down as if his hand was a scanner. Even more unsettling was the man's eyes; they were closed but it felt as if he could sense Tadeo's presence.

"My Lord, Tadeo," the man spoke softly.

"Who are you?" Tadeo cautiously

approached the man. "How do you know my name?"

"Many questions boy, many questions. In time they will be answered. You have my word."

"Where am I?"

"Have patience." The man continued, "you will soon know."

"Why did you refer to me as "Lord?"

"To everyone, but one, you are the Lord of this realm, all realms. Don't you understand? You created us? You have earned my respect, my master.

"Master? Master Tadeo," He said to himself "Is this for real? Cool!"

Tadeo's eyes drew away from the man and came across a pink puddle with shattered glass around it. Spilled puddles of potions, Tadeo assumed. Glass jars were in the corner, several strange looking things were crammed into them. Tadeo saw what looked like various animal body parts - intestines, brains, ears, eye balls and even a tongue.

The urge to vomit rose up but Tadeo had to resist, so he sunk the 'ship' back down into his body. The old man wore red and black robes and had long luscious hair.

"My name is Sliftu, and you are in the labyrinth with the beast," said the old man, introducing himself.

"Beast?"

"A venomous snake, Pupetra's pet. They call it the Bloodthirsty Consumer and that pet cost me everything, it killed my whole family. Pupetra is the root of all evil, she has been the queen of all realms. We have all been under her rule for centuries, but now you can save us all."

"Uh - Okay! But first I just need to get out of here."

"About that, yes, also see the clock up there in the sky," Sliftu pointed up. "That is a countdown, if you don't get out of here before it reaches zero, Pupetra's rule will continue for eternity and you will remain here forever."

"Wait, WHAT?" Tadeo needed his asthma pump right now. He took a few deep breaths which calmed him down a bit.

"But is there a way out of here?" Tadeo asked.

"Well, I suppose. My father's staff, which has unlimited and great power, is guarded by the beast. He told me if I shake the orb staff a map to escape this realm will appear in the orb."

Fear hit Tadeo right in the heart like a punch as he heard the hiss of the beast on the other side of the wall. He had to get to the beast and find that staff. Not wasting any time, with

Sliftu's help, he made a tracking device out of some of the high-tech scraps by Sliftu's feet. Tadeo climbed up the wall, peered over the top and saw the beast. He threw the device towards the beast hoping it would land securely on its back. It did!

Tracking the beast, Tadeo and Sliftu, who was still levitating, eventually found the staff. It had a knife in front of it; very suspicious Tadeo thought as they approached it. Sliftu held the staff and stood on two feet. If put in the wrong hands this staff could cause certain doom Tadeo thought. Sliftu then shook the staff and a map appeared in the orb and they started using this to find the escape tunnel.

Out of the corner of his eye Tadeo noticed a flash of light and then the knife turned miraculously into the beast. Thinking quickly, Sliftu used a spell to create a bubble which made the beast move in slow motion temporarily. It wouldn't hold it for long, he explained, so they both used the advantage this created to run while following the map, which they hoped would lead them quickly out of the labyrinth.

Soon, the spell wore off and the beast started catching up to them, they seemed to be almost on their way out of the realm, they just needed to make it a few more yards. Tadeo and

Sliftu had to go left, right, forward, right, forward, left, right, left, forward, until they lost the beast. They were running for their lives while trying to follow the map to their escape route.

Eventually they came to a point where there were two paths. Sliftu's staff told him to go left, little did they know that the beast was on their right-hand side, smelling their fear, following them all along. They both turned left and gasped as they stood in front of a dead end. According to the map this was the place. They both heard screams of pain and a voice, which Tadeo recognized. Clitho and Barboach, I had completely forgotten about them, Tadeo thought.

"Maybe we have to run through the wall, it's hidden in plain sight." Tadeo got a good run up and ran through the wall like a ghost.

Sliftu began to pace himself and got ready to jump through the wall, but it was too late the beast's poisonous fangs held him back and dug into the skin of his ankle.

Chapter 4

Tadeo found himself hurtling down into a blue pit, he only caught a faint glimpse of where he was because the wind in his face made it impossible for him to see properly and breathe. Everything was a blur that swirled out of existence. The blue pit below seemed to swallow him, and he appeared to be tumbling towards the sea.

He felt like he was suffocating. Tadeo went down at a speed that constricted his throat, so he hardly got a breath. His mouth agape, Tadeo let go instead of trying to fight what was happening, he just let gravity do the rest.

Somehow even through Tadeo's skin he felt the temperature slowly, and effectively, dropping. The sea didn't bring a winter chill like Tadeo was expecting but rather a welcome coolness of an autumn breeze. Every cell in his body was screaming for oxygen.

Tadeo's head emerged from the depths of the deep sea. In the vastness of the ocean it was very easy to lose hope. He would have let his legs dangle, but he was glad he knew how to swim.

The frosty cold water stole heat from his socks, the water surged up his legs. Even his blood felt frozen. Tadeo began to sink, he was breathing rapidly and could hear the sound of oxygen flooding in and out of his lungs.

He turned his head only to be attacked by an oncoming wave, it had a terrifying agile feel to it and the sound of the crashing waves was loud enough to make his head explode.

Tadeo's eyes scanned the horizon and he saw another wave which was drawing closer like wild horses. It wasn't a tsunami but matched the power and intensity of one. The only difference was the wave that approached looked like a medium- sized surfing wave.

The wave hit Tadeo and it felt like a

knockout punch. His whole body turned as if he was in a washing machine and plunged him into darkness.

Tadeo slowly opened his eyes allowing him to jump back to reality. He was on what appeared to be a beach. He arose and heard whispers in the breeze. He looked down and realized his clothes were ripped and damp.

Scrunching his toes, he felt the softness of the sand and only then did he notice that both of his shoes were gone.

"Probably lost at sea," Tadeo told himself.

The shore was turning liquid gold, vivid

in the light. The sight of the sun melting into the sky was a divine painting.

Tadeo squinted his eyes and made out a figure in the distance, who looked very muscular. The figure shot his head to the right and his eyes met Tadeo's. Tadeo immediately knew that this figure was a man.

The figure was walking unusually slowly, almost robotically, as if his brain was struggling to tell each foot to take the next step. Tadeo took a few steps forward until something sharp dug deep into his foot; he fell to the ground. His hand felt something, he tried to pull it out, but it was almost cemented into the sand.

"Let me help you with that," a voice spoke behind Tadeo.

"Yes, please sir," The man's voice was strong and deep. When he took off his hood Tadeo saw the man, it was Nathan, his worst nightmare right in front of him. Tadeo's jaw dropped in shock. He was stronger than I remember in real life, Tadeo thought.

Nathan managed to get the sharp object out of the sand, to both of their disappointment it was only two rulers but had the layout of a cross guard sword.

"Here you go my Lord," Nathan offered it to Tadeo with two hands.

"Thank you," Tadeo replied. "And I don't suppose everyone here refers to me as a Lord?"

"Unfortunately, no." Tadeo noticed Nathan was being very mindful of what he was saying. "Not to most of us,"

"What do you mean?" Tadeo asked "I thought I was like the chosen one."

"That you are Tadeo but…" Nathan spotted a vague shadow in the air.

Nathan yanked Tadeo's arm aggressively and ran. They moved like cheetahs racing through grass, nothing stopped them. They left the beach and ran into what appeared to be a jungle.

Tadeo wanted to scream out in pain, the branches tore his bare arms and legs. With Nathan holding his wrist very tightly he couldn't even feel a pulse for a split-second. It seemed as if Nathan was afraid; running away from something. The thought of Nathan scared puzzled Tadeo. He didn't think he was scared of anything.

The humidity of the jungle made Tadeo feel sick and queasy. He was making a groaning sound that seemed off-putting to Nathan. Tadeo swatted another insect, sweat rolled down his body like melting ice.

He began bouncing slightly, which only wore him out even more. Tadeo was no longer running and began to stumble; he didn't even notice the stinging nettle cut that dug into his skin.

Eventually, they made it to a place which looked like a blacksmith forge.

"Infernore" Nathan said greeting the blacksmith.

"Nathan my boy, how are you?" Infernore was burning coal. "It's been a while," he said, wiping his face with a handkerchief he pulled from his sleeve.

"Yeah," Nathan explained. "But we need

your help,"

"WE!?" Infernore's face looked as hot as the fire behind him. "How many times Nathan have I told you, we can't let anyone know about here. Otherwise we will suffer the wrath of Pupetra!"

Nathan stood aside and Infernore turned his gaze to Tadeo.

"Tadeo," Infernore gasped.

"How do you know my name?" Tadeo asked.

"It's about time he knows what is going on here."

"Yes," Infernore agreed.

"Pupetra was an abandoned puppet that washed upon the shore of this island one day. She was hit with a drop of blood that fell from the sky. Then Pupetra took the form of a human. On the beach she found a purple ring, which generated her power and that was how she rose to rule over this island.

"However, before Pupetra took over she heard that a chosen one would save us all. Somehow, she was able to conjure a cloud and the thunder from it hit everyone above ground. Thankfully, the thunder was harmless, but it erased everyone's memory, so they wouldn't remember that a chosen one was coming."

"Then how come you guys never forgot?" Tadeo asked.

"We were in the tunnels that protected our memory," Nathan told Tadeo.

"Tunnels?" Tadeo looked puzzled.

"Ok, let's get moving. We'll have to explain later. If you are going to defeat Pupetra we need to get you some weapons," Infernore said.

"I've got a weapon," Tadeo pulled out his ruler sword.

"I'll see what I can do." Infernore replied.

Infernore threw the sword into the forge, then handed Tadeo a pistol in the meantime. He noticed that the pistol was loaded with fidget spinners.

It had been five minutes, then Infernore opened the forge and took out the ruler sword. Infernore put the sword on the anvil, applying full force to the hammer as he hit the sword.

"Go on, it's done. Test it on that tree," Infernore suggested.

With barely any power Tadeo's sword almost sliced through the whole tree trunk.

"Tadeo, we've got to start moving, there isn't much time left," Nathan said pointing upwards.

"Oh God! Only 30 minutes," Tadeo was

in shock. “Come on Nathan, let’s go.”

“Take the shortcut, it is easier,” Infernore said, whilst lifting a rock up and exposing a secret passageway.

“Thank you, Infernore,” Tadeo said.

“No problem,” Infernore replied “Also catch.”

Infernore threw Tadeo a satchel which he caught. This is going to make it easier to carry my stuff, Tadeo was grateful.

Their feet were kissing the sandstone coloured concrete in the tunnel. Tadeo was breathing steadily and started running faster in the tunnel. They had to move fast.

The tunnel was short, but it got them behind the closest tree to the stairs which would lead them to the top of the mountain. They both knew many dangers would be above those stairs, but they had to take a chance.

The stairs were in a twisted spiral and had the colour of antique cream. A lot of dust battled with Tadeo's asthma. Once they reached the peak of the mountain the sight was horrendous.

A woman, who Tadeo assumed was Pupetra, was wearing black dragon skin as a cloak.

"Tadeo," Pupetra muttered through

gritted teeth.

Pupetra had a button for an eye and had tiger claw marks tattooed all over her. She also had a prosthetic left arm.

Her hand moved like a conductor in an orchestra. Moshes, (half monkey, half fishes) sapes, (half spider, half ape) eaions, (half eagle, half lion) cabbits, (half cat, half rabbit), locodiles (half lizard, half crocodile), scorpitrons (scorpion robots), minatours and cyclops all rose from the ground.

Tadeo took out his fidget spinner pistol (FSP) and fired at will. Little did Tadeo know that it was specially made, the red fidget spinners could become fire and blue ones could turn into water. The moshes were destroyed with a single hit of the gun; time was running out!

Nathan was using his Kung Fu skills to lead most of the sapes and cabbits towards the cliff. He front-flipped over all of them and then pushed them off the mountain.

Tadeo threw Nathan his ruler sword and with it he destroyed the minatours and the cyclops. Kicking all the scorpitrons out of his way, Tadeo fired a blast of fire from his FSP but was blocked by the hand of a locodile who had surrounded Nathan without him knowing by camouflaging into the grass.

Tadeo made a full thrust for the locodiles hitting them in the face then getting out his FSP to finish the job. Nathan looked beat down, but he was determined to end this. All that remained were a few sapes, bulloxs and eaions which Tadeo took out with his FSP.

"Surrender Pupetra!" Nathan yelled.

"Never!" She roared.

A bolt of fire hit Nathan across the face, which made him look like he was a blacksmith. Falling to the ground Nathan burned, from the inside!

His bones and organs burned away until he was nothing but dust.

"How's that, supposed chosen one," Pupetra laughed wickedly.

She began conjuring a red cloud from Nathan's dust, but within a split second Pupetra's hand was on the ground, she was so busy conjuring up the cloud she hadn't realised that Tadeo had quickly attacked her with the ruler sword.

The impact of the ruler sword was so deadly Pupetra didn't even feel the pain of her hand getting sliced off. Blood was escaping her body quickly, leaving her body like a waterfall.

Then she disintegrated into the island. As she disappeared a vortex appeared in front of him and with just seconds left on the clock Tadeo was whisked away. Tadeo had made it! He was never so happy to see his room again, sighing in relief.

Tadeo grabbed his controller and logged onto his account. Then remembering to remove the USB he unplugged it from the Gamechip 64.

***

It was Monday morning, five minutes before line-up. In the playground Tadeo's eyes searched for Nathan. His eyes found Nathan underneath the Willow tree with Scott and Callum. Taking a deep breath in and out Tadeo walked towards him.

Scott and Callum went towards the wooden goalposts to play football, leaving Nathan alone. With his shoulders back and chest out Tadeo found himself a shoulder–width apart from Nathan.

"What?" Nathan said, like he was pressed for time.

"I just wanted to say that your ideas for the game were really cool." Tadeo told him.

"Really?" Nathan gave Tadeo a puzzled look.

"Yes, I think we are going to ace this project." Tadeo continued. "Honestly Nathan, you had some great ideas."

"Thanks, man." Nathan thanked him, whilst extending his hand.

And Tadeo firmly shook it.

First lesson of the day was computing, and it was time for Tadeo and Nathan to present their game. When their names were called to present their game, sniggers were detected from all around the room.

"Tadeo, take off your Halloween costume it isn't until October," Ryan shouted at Tadeo.

"You lack the brains to make a Halloween costume Ryan," Tadeo fired at Ryan.

"Brains aren't everything Ryan, in your case they're nothing," Nathan backed Tadeo up.

The whole class burst out laughing. Dead silence fell from Ryan. Nathan managed to give Tadeo a faint smile. After Tadeo sniggered himself, he returned the smile to Nathan.

"It's fine, for every minute I stand here those are minutes off your lunch break." Mrs Crilger said calmly.

"Sorry miss," Rachel apologised on behalf of the class.

"This game is hard guys, believe me I know," Tadeo explained "So, who wants to go first?"

The End

… for now!

Printed in Great Britain
by Amazon